Dear parents, caregivers, and educators:

If you want to get your child excited about reading, you've come to the right place! Ready-to-Read *GRAPHICS* is the perfect launchpad for emerging graphic novel readers.

All Ready-to-Read *GRAPHICS* books include the following:

- ★ **A how-to guide to reading graphic novels for first-time readers**

- ★ **Easy-to-follow panels to support reading comprehension**

- ★ **Accessible vocabulary to build your child's reading confidence**

- ★ **Compelling stories that star your child's favorite characters**

- ★ **Fresh, engaging illustrations that provide context and promote visual literacy**

Wherever your child may be on their reading journey, Ready-to-Read *GRAPHICS* will make them giggle, gasp, and want to keep reading more.

Blast off on this starry adventure . . . a universe of graphic novel reading awaits!

RED TITAN

AND THE NEVER-ENDING MAZE

SIMON SPOTLIGHT

An imprint of Simon & Schuster Children's Publishing Division
1230 Avenue of the Americas, New York, New York 10020
This Simon Spotlight edition December 2021
Text by Arie Kaplan

For more information about special discounts for bulk purchases, please contact
Simon & Schuster Special Sales at 1-866-506-1949 or business@simonandschuster.com.
Manufactured in the United States of America 1121 LAK
2 4 6 8 10 9 7 5 3 1
ISBN 978-1-6659-0182-6 (hc)
ISBN 978-1-6659-0181-9 (pbk)
ISBN 978-1-6659-0183-3 (ebook)

pocket.watch

RYAN'S WORLD

RED TITAN

AND THE NEVER-ENDING MAZE

by **RYAN KAJI**
written by **ARIE KAPLAN**
illustrated by **SHANE L. JOHNSON**

Ready-to-Read *GRAPHICS*

Simon Spotlight
New York   London   Toronto   Sydney   New Delhi

HOW TO READ THIS BOOK

Ryan is here to give you some tips
on reading this book.

It was the end of the day. Red Titan had just finished his last job.

But...

WHOOSH

This wall does not have a weak spot.

This wall sounds different. Maybe it is a weak spot!

Red Titan has saved the day!